Merrily

Daniel Dickson-LaPrade

Published by Daniel Dickson-LaPrade, 2024.

MERRILY

First edition. May 29, 2024.

ISBN: 979-8227487216

Written by Daniel Dickson-LaPrade.

1.

It's taken her half the night, but she's finally gotten inside. The house is silent and dark. She's still wet from the rain and exhausted, and her teeth chatter. She stands at the top of the basement stairs, shivering, listening. Not a sound. She closes the door and steps back down the stairs, leaving her muddy shoes above so she can grab them in a hurry if she needs to. She leaves the light off. She won't have any lights once she hits the sleeper's room and she wants to be able to function in darkness. Besides, there is the guard outside to think about. Using the moonlight filtering through the two small windows near the basement ceiling, she stumbles over to the laundry sink in the corner and washes the thick, cold mud off her hands, taking care not to actually look at her hands as she does so. She turns the tap off again and listens. Pads back up the stairs, opens the basement door, listens some more. Not a sound. The kitchen emerges slowly from the blackness. Rustic wooden table and chairs, simultaneously homey and modern. A kitchen island with pots and pans hanging overhead. The wind outside rattles the odd bone windchime that she saw earlier. She listens for a moment longer and is satisfied. It's time to get to work.

She pads up the stairs to Aaron Vintner's bedroom. The stairs are, thankfully, carpeted, and she is light enough not to cause much creaking. Vintner is her client, though he doesn't know it, and perhaps never will. A friend of his hired her—the same friend who cautioned her to skip the seventh stair up, which she does, to avoid the gunshot bang it makes at the slightest provocation. Vintner's ex-wife apparently only wanted him for his money and was not shy about telling him so at the end of their marriage. There are square and rectangular pale spots on the wall by the staircase where their pictures used to hang. Mara feels a pang at this. She knows all about bad breakups. Could write an entire book on the subject, in fact. But that was why she'd been hired— to help him.

On the second floor, more of the same soft carpeting, and a pair of pictureless walls framing the dark hallway. She passes a spare bedroom, an office with a disused elliptical trainer, a junk room where some sort of remodeling is underway during the daylight hours. Vintner's master bedroom lies at the end of the hall, door half-shut. She drifts to the doorway and listens some more, the quality of the silence already telling her that he is asleep. She lets her head float around the side of the door, noiseless as a shadow, and watches him sleep in what little moonlight the curtains allow in. At his feet, on the wall next to her, a huge mahogany entertainment center, now emitting nothing but the odor of satisfied wealth. Over his head, an immense Kandinsky print. She walks up to the side of his bed, feeling the rhythm of his breathing with her entire body. He looks like a dentist or a CPA, somebody dependable and hard-working and just happening to enjoy a job that makes lots of money. The kind of fellow who goes deep-sea fishing and has opinions about what parts of various European countries have the best wine. He probably flies a small airplane in his spare time. He's on the older side but handsome. What little is visible of his shoulder in the dim light suggests a man who takes care of himself. She is surprised to notice such unprofessional thoughts about a client. Then again, it's been a while.

Hanging from her shoulder, her work bag. She pulls out a wooden tube just larger than a lipstick, uncaps it, puts it to her lips, and blows a puff of blue vapor over Vintner's sleeping head. He grunts softly, shifts a bit, and falls into even deeper sleep. Then she pulls the handkerchief out of her bag, along with the vial of pale blue glass wrapped in it. Unstopping the vial, she tips it onto the handkerchief, then replaces the lid. The smell of the stuff—unlike any other smell in her experience—can only be described as *blue*, though her chemist has also smuggled in hints of other odors that will trigger useful associations in her sleeper's mind—here a hint of Victoria's Secret perfume, there a bit of hot drier lint, and also faint traces of—cedar? She places the half-wadded handkerchief a few inches in front of Vintner's sleep-gaped mouth. There is an art to this: too close, and the vapors from the handkerchief knock the sleeper out entirely, and prevent proper dreaming; too far, and the sleeper will be disturbed by the new person joining him in his bed. Then there is the degree of bunched-up-ness of the handkerchief, which affects the liquid's evaporation time, and the amount of liquid used, and the weight of the dreamer, and a dozen other factors. But Hugh, her mentor, has taught her well, and she has done this many times before. Without a conscious thought, she places the handkerchief in precisely the right spot, down to the centimeter, and waits in the way that an elderly spider waits.

Vintner now sleeps deeply and will soon begin the kind of dreaming useful to her. She silently removes her baggy sweater and the enormous purse that serves as her work bag and places both on the floor right outside the doorway, pausing to take a smallish wooden box out of her bag. The sliding lid reveals a two-inch-high wooden doll, crude and vague in its features, little more than a squat cylinder turned on a lathe with bulges for head, bust, and hips, resting upon a wide, flat platform that allows it to stand stably. It has been painted to have Mara's dark, wavy hair and grey-green clothes, though wear has begun to fade the colors and wear down the bulges.

She is lucky tonight. Vintner is sleeping close to one edge of his bed, rather than right in the center, and is, moreover, facing the wall. Mara places the doll on the bed between the two pillows, about a foot behind Vintner's head, and gently gets into the bed behind him, alert to any changes in his breathing. By now, the various scents in the handkerchief's vapors should be triggering associations in Vintner's memory that will give her material to work with. As the warmth of the room, the softness of the bed, and the distant handkerchief's vapors make her drowsy, she grabs the handkerchief, inhales deeply from it, and replaces it in exactly the same spot in front of Vintner's face. She gazes in front of her at the tiny doll, barely visible in the moonlight. And far, far beyond the doll, the back of Aaron Vintner's sleeping head, miles and miles away. As her breath blows past the doll to the dreaming man's head, her eyelids droop, drift dozily downwards, then close entirely.

2.

She falls for a while without actually falling. No color, no sound, no feeling, no self, beyond all time, and ignorant of space. A featureless ocean of darkness. A vague thing like a memory begins to form in response to this blackness, and a thought comes: *I am seeing this darkness.* And another, and another: *I am not this darkness. This darkness is separate from me. I am Mara, and I am experiencing the Great Dark.*

The blackness continues, but now there is a vague sense of time, and of motion. Mara can feel the empty space all around her for tens of thousands of miles on a side, soundless, boundless, featureless, blank. Continuing forward through this dark sea, she notices a space far, far ahead where the darkness is a bit less dark. After a few eons, a tiny star becomes visible to her in the far distance. She draws closer, still entombed in silence, remembering her training: *I am Mara, moving through the Great Dark.* The star expands slowly into a disc, a ball, a glowing sphere dozens or hundreds or thousands of miles across, effulgent in the dead silence. Coming still closer, she sees, as always, that the ball of light is a blindingly bright center surrounded by a sphere of rounded cubes thousands of miles across, cubes of various sizes and colors, each containing memories, concepts, associations. Each of these miles-wide cubes with rounded corners holds an image: a faded bookstore, seen from a height of two or three feet, filled with Star Wars merchandise; an old dining room with cheap vinyl flooring and a pleasing warmth and safety; a swing set under a cloudy sky, a sense of menace thick in the blue-grey cube holding the picture. These cells hold the detritus that is just barely, and only partially, available to conscious awareness, the materials through which pain and lust and guilt and misery percolate to pass into the dreamer's mind and produce narrative.

After surveying the deep blue cubes and the yellowish orange cubes and the deathly grey cubes, the pictures of old homes and old toys and old friends, she flexes her mind and dives between the massive cuboidal cells and into the glowing center of the sphere. Between the sphere of colored memories and the glowing star in the middle, a vast expanse of space, seemingly thousands of miles deep—though with a practiced flexing of her mind, she crosses this distance in moments. Vintner has already begun to dream. A few gelatinous cubes around the periphery are already extending long tendrils to the center, which is a rippling ball of silvery liquid. This silvery ball, Vintner's dreaming mind, is drawing the nearest tendrils from the outside together into a coherent world, a coherent story, just as it does with sensory impressions and ideas when waking. But since the inner sphere is drawing together tendrils from memories and instincts rather than from things perceived outside, the resulting coherence can only be the coherence of a story, not the coherence of a reality. Each single event now dawning in the dreamer's mind makes sense in light of the one before it and will make sense in light of the one to follow, but the people and places and objects will shift and dissolve and reform without the dreamer's half-active mind ever noticing.

For a while, Mara turns her attention once again to the outer sphere of gelatinous cubes. It will be some time before the dream-narrative really gets started, and seeing the relative sizes, shapes, and colors of major memories will be useful once she begins to actually change the dream. She starts by looking at the cells already trying to get themselves knotted into the dream's tapestry, the memories trying to press tendrils into the dreamer's mind. As she expects, one of these cells contains a movie of the man's dog, a worried-looking golden retriever just starting to get some grey whiskers. Another cell, an awful grey miasma, contains the startling blast of mocking laughter that Vintner heard over the phone when his wife told him about the death of this dog. Occasionally, this grey memory is rippled with bright pinks and oranges, as though a chance firing of Vintner's neurons was bringing it back to life in spite of the man's best efforts never to think it again. The ropy fiber extending out of this cell thrashes with an awful energy all its own, and its coloring is flashing ever faster and more brightly. Mara can tell exactly what the contours of the nightmare are going to be. She darts down to the center of the dream, the silver ball attracting the tendrils to itself in a sort of snake-dance. The dog tendril is already just touching the central ball at one tiny point, but the laughter tendril is less direct, whipping this way and that way like a headless serpent. The silvery sphere of Vintner's mind ripples in response to this serpent, and the ripples do not look healthy. The dream is already starting, and though it is not yet a full-blown nightmare, it is clear where things are headed.

Mara presses the laughing-wife tendril away from the surface of Vintner's mind, coaxing it gently and from the side so that it does not notice and attempt to push back. There is only so much that she can learn from the outside of the dream, and if Vintner's mind is already attracting nightmare ingredients, it is only a matter of time until another laughter-tentacle or something equally terrible presses itself into the sphere in the center. Without her, Vintner will just have another trauma-dream, retracing and intensifying old pain. She will have to go down into his dream with him and see the story from his point of view, guiding it along other channels, attracting other tendrils to it, giving it the ability to heal him instead of wounding him afresh. With a feeling much like holding her breath, Mara dives into the ball of silvery liquid in the center and opens her—or rather, Vintner's—eyes.

3.

For a few moments, everything is jumbled together. Mara can still see, thousands of miles above and all around, the outer sphere of multicolored memory-cells, a few of them sending down strands to take part in the dream. Below her and beginning to envelop her, the silvery ball of the dreamer's mind. But she can also see what Vinter is seeing: a wooden staircase, a strip of ancient carpet down its middle, leading down to a basement with a concrete floor. In fact, she realizes, this is the same basement where she recently washed mud from her hands and left her filthy shoes. It looks so different in the daytime! With difficulty, she adjusts her fit to Vinter's mind so that the sphere of memories outside disappears, and she is dreaming right along with him.

She can "hear" his thoughts, so to speak, just as he can, and she can also "feel" the emotional valence of things. She and Vintner are terrified. Something is wrong. They rush down the remaining steps into the basement in their shared dream-body, frantically searching for Betsy, the golden retriever. They can hear the occasional click-click-click of her claws on the floor but can't find where the sound is coming from. They can smell her, even—a real oddity in dreams, where vision and hearing are usually the only senses—but they can't find her *anywhere*. A mounting sense that something terrible has happened, is happening, will happen fills the basement in which they search, looking in vain behind the laundry hamper and the laundry sink and the unused weight-bench with its freight of folded towels. Vintner looks up at the pair of basement windows near the ceiling—perhaps Betsy is actually outside? —and Mara realizes where the dream is heading. She saw the memory-cell of these very basement windows earlier, in her tour of Vintner's outer sphere of memories. The dog will appear at this window, she realizes, and will run away or vanish or be yanked away by force. The ex-wife's laughter, chilling and callous, will make the dog's doom obvious, and the nightmare will kick Vintner back into traumatized wakefulness. Knocking away the laughter-tendril earlier has only delayed the inevitable climax: like train-tracks, Vintner's mind will always lead him along old agonies and traumas to the same awful moment. She has to work fast.

Mara pulls herself free of Vintner's mind, watching the silvery globe recede beneath her, the center of a writhing mass of tendrils—dog and evil laughter and basement window. She speeds to the outer sphere of memories, skimming along in search of warm, joyous memories—they will be yellowish-pink or pale orange, like an apricot or a peach—involving times when Vintner's love for his wife had not yet become sodden with horror and poison. Finally, she has it: Silvie, Vintner's ex-wife, looking up bashfully from under her bangs, embarrassed, vulnerable, gorgeous. How young she looks! The memory has become connected to all the later and more horrible memories of their doomed romance and hellish marriage, so that every time his mind has found this rare sanctuary of happiness, it has been pulled automatically to dread and horror. She'll have to be careful in using this memory: already, its connection to later events is greying its corners, causing it to be the same sort of cancerous misery that the bad memories are. Briefly, she considers appearing as Silvie in Vintner's dream, entering the tendril of this Silvie-memory and working the ex-wife like a puppet. But never having met the girl, she wouldn't be able to do the job convincingly, and besides, with how poisoned Vintner's mind is against his ex-wife, such a gambit might be risky. She remembers an old piece of advice from when Hugh had first started mentoring her: "the best face to be wearing in someone else's dream is their own thoughts, or the weather."

Working quickly, Mara presses against this jellied cube rhythmically until its sides become more liquid, more malleable. She then rubs the surface of the cell until a small bulb can be shaped from the side, a bulb which she then grips with both hands, pulling gently so as not to break the tendril. She flies down to the center of the dreamer's mind as quickly as she dares and sees that she is almost too late: already the Betsy tendril and the basement-window tendril have found each other and coiled together, their shared tip nearly touching the rippling, unquiet surface of the silver sphere in the center. Meanwhile, the evil-laughter tendril thrashes just above the surface, ever closer to penetrating the nightmare and bringing it to its climax. Mara drops the bashful-Silvie tendril a moment so that she can pry the dog-memory and the window-memory apart. She then flings herself into the evil-laughter tendril, causing it to thrash away for the time being. She grabs the bashful-Silvie tendril again before it can retract into its home, presses it into the surface of the dream, and dives back into the silvery ball.

Vintner has just heard an unexpected sound and, with a burst of hope, has turned to look up at the basement window expecting to see his beloved dog. But instead of Betsy, Vintner-and-Mara see Silvie peering in. Noticing that she has been seen, Silvie dips her head demurely, a tad embarrassed. So young! Like a young girl caught doing something naughty. But the sight of Silvie has already given Vintner a dark feeling in his stomach, a sense of impending doom. To counteract this, Mara makes herself gasp, playacting astonishment at the face in the window. The shared dream-body takes up that gasp, transmitting its sudden astonishment to Vintner. Then Mara says in her mind, as loudly and clearly as she can, in as neutral a voice as she can manage, "Silvie's been trying to see me without my clothes on!" Instinctively, Vintner looks down at his crotch, taking Mara's gaze with him. And there it is—he is not wearing pants, and his naked penis, an erect pink flagpole, is plainly exposed, revealed by Mara's suggestion. Mara controls her breathing as best she can and drags their shared gaze back up to the window. Silvie's embarrassed face has begun to shift to something more darkly amused; behind her, the sun has disappeared from the sky. Mara doesn't have to leave the dream to know that the bad laughter is again finding the dream's surface and attempting to burrow inside. "She's a peeping Tom, and she's trespassing!" Mara thinks with indignation. She furrows their shared brow and puffs out their shared chest. "The police are going to catch her for sure and take her off to jail!" Then Mara dives back out of the dream again to find the materials that she needs for the dream's new climax.

As she expected, her mention of the police and jail has awakened a variety of half-remembered crime dramas, as well as an ill-fated fraternity party two decades previous. She finds two forbidding uniformed cops in mirrored sunglasses and brings their tendril back down to the dream itself, pressing it first against the side of the embarrassed-Silvie tendril and then against the wall of the dream. The Betsy tendril, meanwhile, is floating about uncertainly near the surface of the dream, still feeling a need to participate but no longer having any obvious role to play. Mara shoves this dog-tendril into the side of the staircase tendril at just the point where it meets the surface of the silvery globe, then dives back inside to make sure her conclusion takes hold.

As soon as she plunges back into Vintner's dream-body, Mara notices that the sky outside is dim, the color in the basement is dim, and the chest and stomach she is sharing with Vintner are tightened with a grim mixture of anger and satisfaction. *Serves the bitch right*, Vintner is thinking, a horde of awful memories called to the dream by his wrath—including the memory of that awful laughter. In any dream, a mental association is a mental event is a real event. Any moment, Silvie will break free, or there will be a tape recording that she has made, or in some other way the laughter will get back in to destroy Mara's progress. Mara parries the laughter-tendril without even needing to see it, instinctively, by closing their shared eyes for just a moment and calling up a visual memory of Silvie looking embarrassed and peering in through the basement window. Momentarily distracted by the light warmth of the image, Vintner's sleeping mind lets go of his belly and chest, which Mara hurriedly empties of all air and uses to inhale a full, normal breath. Then she plants another thought: "She looks for all the world like she's been caught jerking off!" Then she laughs, hard, theatrically, with her belly, and opens her eyes. The sun is shining in through the window again, and some color has started coming back into the basement. "Now where in the hell could that blasted DOG have gotten off to?" Pulling without seeming to pull, with long-practiced subtlety, Mara manages to drag their shared head and torso around to look back up the basement stairs. And there, three steps above them, is the dog, waiting patiently with her usual expression of puzzled concern. *Betsy!* the man shouts, and he jumps up the stairs so suddenly that he leaves Mara behind, so that she again finds herself floating free, the silvery ball of the dream below her, the tendrils slowing their motion and beginning to thin, to retract, as Vintner's mind prepares to return to dreamless sleep.

There is just one more thing to do, though it isn't important. Really, it doesn't have anything to do with helping Vintner, either. He will likely never know that Mara was hired or what she has done for him. Nevertheless, she can't leave a dream she's shaped without signing her work. She has to leave her mark, even if the dreamer forgets all about it upon waking. In the past, she's relied on puns, or on side characters sharing her name or face. Hugh Benson—or Hugh Tensile, as all their friends knew him—was always fond of wordplay and anagrams, the more elliptical the better. For a while, a commercial from the Sara Lee pie company was on TV all the time, and many dreamers had a clear enough memory that with a little splicing, she could replay it as her signature: "Nobody doesn't like Mara Lee!"

But with how rapidly this dream is concluding, she doesn't have time to get fancy. She searches a continent of older memories that have the air of carefree triviality—smaller, warmly colored cells faded to marshmallowy pastels—until she finds the two memories that she is looking for: a memory of an ice cream truck and a memory of singing "Row, Row, Row Your Boat" with other kids, apparently at church camp. She hurriedly teases a tendril from each memory, winds them together, and flies them down to the surface of the dream, which is already becoming smooth, inert, and dark, penetrated only by tendrils involving Betsy and the basement stairs. The composite childhood memory of an ice cream truck playing the old song will add a pleasant touch of innocence to the final moments of the dream. Mara presses the spliced tendril gently into the dream's surface and, her signature completed, hurtles back upward, toward and through Vintner's universe of multicolored memories to the great blackness beyond.

4.

After an eternity in mindless darkness, the scent of Vintner's sleeping body and his bedroom began trickling back to her as she drifted through the small wooden doll back into herself. Still sedated by the handkerchief's fumes, she felt half-dead, her brain hopelessly foggy, her limbs unfeeling sticks. She shouldn't have gone through with the job tonight, as tired as she was. Dealing with the cops, getting into Vintner's house—it was a wonder she hadn't just slept like a log until he woke up. Mara took a deep breath. Another. Next to her, Vintner grunted, shifted. She held as still as a corpse until his breathing settled back into deeper sleep. As her limbs tingled back to life, she reached into her pocket for the special inhaler she'd gotten from her chemist. She took a silent puff from the plastic disk, held it in for a moment, released it, then replaced the inhaler in her pocket. Her heart began beating faster, and her whole body began tingling with a twitchy sort of wakefulness.

She was surprised to find herself aroused. This was not uncommon—she had taken part in more than a few sex-dreams, after all—but the most recent dream was not exactly a bodice-ripper. She remembered looking down at Vintner's erect cock with their shared eyes and swallowed. In the bedroom's dim light, she saw that his sheet had slid down partially, revealing his chest and part of his belly. He was no Adonis, but there was muscle there, and she could see the faint outlines of his abs. Fully awake, she peered at the muscles of his belly. Moving slowly, she pressed the edge of the sheet an inch to the side so that she could see more of them, could glimpse a narrow trail of dark hair that began just below his navel and disappeared under the sheet below. *This is wrong*, she thought. *This is a client, and he doesn't even know he's a client. This is wrong for me to do.* She let her eyes drift up his chest, his hard, rounded shoulders, the firm line of his jaw. She could lie here for a few more moments, surely, and just enjoy the smell of his body. She silently grabbed her handkerchief and doll and put them into her pockets. Idly, she wondered how his ass would look. *I've got to leave.*

She drifted from the bed. God, he was handsome. She considered staying for a few moments longer enjoying his scent, but her habits came to her aid. Without thinking, she was already shifting her eyes over to her jacket, still slung over the back of a chair, then all around the bedroom to make sure she hadn't left anything behind. Something caught her eye and she glanced at the window. Sitting very still on the edge of the windowsill was the shadow of a woman with no woman there.

Mara grabbed her jacket and bag and sprinted down the stairs two and three at a time, not caring about noise, nearly falling, ran through the kitchen to the basement doorway. She grabbed her shoes and hit the back door, open, out, closed the door behind her, ran through rain-wet mud in socked feet. Thankfully, she saw no sign of the guard. She ran to a side corner of the yard to a pair of birch trees, one on each side of the wooden fence. Behind her, she heard the back door open and close, and knew without looking that the Silhouette was mimicking the same movements that she had made in leaving the house, was sprinting across the yard just as she had. Mara jumped at the nearest birch tree, gripped it in her arms, and shimmied four feet up its rough trunk, scraping herself on the paper-white bark. As the Silhouette's muddy, shlucking footfalls came closer, Mara got one foot on top of the wooden fence and clumsily tossed herself to the other birch tree, then hopped down to the mud on the other side. To her left was a hole in the ground nearly three feet wide, an immense pile of mud, a disused umbrella with one of its bones broken, the membrane fluttering. As she heard the Silhouette scrabble up the tree and moan in pain from the birch bark, just as she had done, Mara sprinted down a wet, grassy incline to the sidewalk below.

Vintner's house was at the end of a cul-de-sac. She ran up the sidewalk through rain-puddles and the dim cones of light from streetlamps, shoes in hand, until she reached a side-street. She hurriedly shod herself, then took off running again. She wondered how she had picked up a Silhouette. They usually formed when some dream-content in the sleeper's mind made an accidental connection with something in the weaver's mind. Returning from the dream, the weaver would bring back some shard of common meaning that took human form, and that would then follow the weaver for hours, or until it could be shaken off, or until it killed and replaced the weaver. But what could have connected to Mara's mind? She had never owned a dog. She'd had a relationship or two end badly before, but—

Turning right onto Gray Street, she finally had her bearings. Spending all her time in dreams as she did, she found the inflexible rectangular geography of waking life confusing. She turned onto Pickard, then took another right onto Main. Risking a glimpse behind her, she saw that the Silhouette was already developing wavy, dark hair and a baggy olive drab jacket. Before too much longer, it was going to have a face, as well. Hers.

On either side of Main Street were the darkened windows of smallish stores, offices for lawyers and accountants, a barber shop, a tag agency, a small dental practice. Half a block ahead was the three-story building where she was headed, the tallest building for miles around. At one in the morning, the building was dark except for the top floor, the bar where people in her line of work hung out, lit by a pink neon sign that read THE GLUESHINE, the final E of which had burned out several years previous. Above the odd words was a crude neon picture of a horse walking unsteadily on its hind legs, a jug of XXX-brand moonshine dangling from its front hoof, an odd look of desperate sadness on its face. She had slowed to a jog despite her terror and was gasping frantically. Ten yards or so behind her she heard the Silhouette aping her breathing and pace. Soon, she knew, the Silhouette would become more *mentally* like her as well, predicting her movements and plans. She had to reach the Glueshine so one of her fellow weavers could help her, or a chemist, or the cheerless doorman—somebody who would know what a Silhouette was, and what to do about it. As she ran, she dug furiously in her immense purse.

Her side pricked by pain, her breath coming in gasps that didn't get her enough air, she finally reached the glass double doors of the lobby and barreled inside. On her left and right were the glass walls of a chiropractor's clinic and a shoe store for people with more money than taste, both closed. She ran to the elevator at the end of the lobby and jabbed the up arrow, finally finding the zip ties she'd been digging for in her purse. As the elevator doors opened, the Silhouette came panting through the glass double doors and sprinted the length of the lobby. Mara dove inside the elevator and stabbed the 3 button, then the two arrows pointing at one another that symbolized closing doors. The greyish and indistinct woman shape that matched Mara breath for breath put its hand between the closing doors and joined Mara inside the elevator. She and Mara exchanged identical nervous glances, the Silhouette's lips gaining in redness and shape, the folds of her jacket becoming less vague and shadowy with each second. Finally, the elevator doors slid closed.

5.

Mara moved. She kicked the Silhouette's shin, gave the Silhouette the hardest open-handed slap she could, and sent it colliding with the side wall of the elevator. Stunned and wrong-footed, the Silhouette tried to catch up and mimic her movements, but Mara was already grabbing it by one wrist and shoving it against the front wall of the elevator. Finally, the elevator began its slow climb upward. A vicious punch to the kidney, then another, and she was able to grab the thing's other wrist, get a zip tie out, and bind the Silhouette's hands behind its back. The Silhouette tried to cry out, tried to say what Mara would say: "Stop, you're hurting me!" But the voice was vague and muffled and wispy, and sent chills up Mara's spine. "Shut up!" she shouted, and immediately realized her mistake: now the thing had heard her voice.

The moment the doors opened, Mara shoved the Silhouette out, noticing as she did so that it already had her fingernails, the crosshatched scars on her left wrist, her bracelet. "You won't get away with this, bitch!" said the other Mara, and now its voice was clear, and hers. She had to get the other Mara to the Glueshine. It was as tall and as clever and as strong as she was now, and only her zip ties were saving her from a mirror-image fight that neither of them could win.

As the doors closed behind them, Mara realized that the third floor seemed oddly dark. Then she saw that the Glueshine was nowhere to be seen. Instead, there was an accountant's office on her right and a travel agency on her left. Directly in front of her, where the dark entrance of the bar should have been, was a music supply store, its window crowded with "gently used" musical instruments and advertisements for private lessons. As the other Mara tried to wriggle free, she realized that she was on the second floor, not the third. Her doppelganger must have hit the 2 button during their struggle. To make matters worse, there was a light on in the accountant's office. Inside, a middle-aged man with dark hair and wire-frame glasses sat at a desk looking into a book on his left and writing important things from it into the book on his right. Because the lobby was so much dimmer than his desk, he wouldn't be able to easily see through the office's glass wall even if he were to look up. Mara tripped the Silhouette and pressed her against the glass, keeping her hand over the woman's mouth without getting bitten. The other Mara whimpered and thrashed, but the trick seemed to be working. With each passing second, the Silhouette's breathing became more uncertain, her sweater tighter and darker, her hair straighter and shorter, her chest and shoulders broader. Unable to see Mara, it was now trying to become more like the handsome man in the suit in front of it. And then the man looked up. Peered. Mara kicked one of the Silhouette's feet out from under it and began dragging it back towards the elevator. The man's mouth fell open and he dropped his pencil. Stood. Mouthed the word "Hey!"

Mara dragged her Silhouette back to the elevator and stabbed the UP button as the man ran to the glass door of the office. Thankfully the elevator hadn't left, and the doors opened immediately. She tripped the Silhouette again and dragged it inside, keeping it facing away from her. The man, well over six feet tall and broad-shouldered, ran through the glass door and reached the elevator just after its doors closed. Then the Silhouette, thrashing furiously, screamed "Daddy!"

6.

The Silhouette was now taller, bulkier, and stronger than she was. Mara was only able to keep it moving toward the entrance of the Glueshine by holding its wrists high behind it and kicking at its feet occasionally to trip it up. "Let me *go*!" it snarled in a raspy contralto. "I want to see my *Dad*!" Mara kept shoving and tripping until they were face-to-face with the immense, baby-headed bouncer, whose bored look indicated that he had seen this exact situation unfold on at least three dozen previous occasions and had used the same remedy successfully for each.

Out of breath, arms in agony from keeping the larger woman in check, Mara simply gasped "Silhouette." The bouncer—his name was Mike, she now remembered, because of course it was—produced the noncommittal grunt that he used instead of language and put a bludgeon-fingered hand delicately on the Silhouette's shoulder, guiding it away, silent and unprotesting, through a side door that Mara had never noticed before.

The Glueshine would be closing in an hour, and this being a weeknight, only every third table held customers. She walked slowly, catching her breath, to the large picture window that took up one side of the bar, then plopped down into a booth. What a nightmare. She'd brought a meaning-connection back from Vintner's dream, had allowed it to mirror her almost completely, and had even drawn the attention of some nameless clerk or accountant whom, she now realized, probably thought that he had witnessed a kidnapping, and had probably seen that the elevator took them to the third floor. Sure enough, glancing over her shoulder she saw Mike the bouncer raise a single calming-but-threatening-but-mainly-calming hand to the tall man in suit and glasses now shouting at him just outside the bar's entrance. Mara whipped her head around and dug in her purse, finally locating a yellow muslin scarf and a pair of cheap shades that she had absolutely no recollection of owning. As she finished knotting her scarf old-lady-in-the-rain style under her chin, a blonde woman with lipstick the color of beef liver strode over to take her order. "Gin greyhound," Mara half-whispered, and risked another look over her shoulder. Mike's hand had drifted an inch higher than it was before, hinting subtly that injuries were a specialty, while the man in the suit had shifted gears to calm, half-apologetic reasoning.

Mara faced front again, sighed, pulled a pack of Pall Mall filterless out of her purse, and placed it mechanically on the table next to her napkin and utensils. The waitress set down a smallish glass with alcohol-flavored ice water in it and a green plastic basket filled with albino tortilla chips. The waitress, whom Mara didn't recognize, peered at her. "Mara Lee? You okay, honey? You look like you've seen a ghost!" The waitress placed a hand gently on Mara's shoulder.

"I'm fine," said Mara, managing a wan smile. The hand didn't leave her shoulder. "Thank you," she said finally. The waitress evaporated and Mara looked out the picture window at the town below. Smallish office buildings and shops nearby, lines of identical ticky-tacky houses further out, and beyond that, the cluster of tallish buildings that made up the university. She shook out a cigarette and lit it with one of the bar's matchbooks. With a bit of concentration, she was able to get it after only three tries. As drizzle streaked the window, she smoked and thought and regretted. After a while, she felt eyes on her and looked over. Toward the middle of the bar sat an older man with silvery hair watching her expressionlessly. He looks almost like Hugh, she thought. The man, having seen what he'd wanted to see, went back to his drink. Mara continued watching him a few seconds more, a sad and wistful gaze that she felt hardening into a glare.

Mike appeared suddenly next to her. Outside his usual spot by the bar's entrance, he looked enormous, like a minotaur. His face had no real use for fancy things like expressions and didn't bother using one now. He spent a moment looking at her blankly as his mouth put some words together. "It's took care of," he said with a meaningless nod, then wandered off, carried by the same mysterious geological forces that had brought him.

As her cigarette dwindled away the minutes, she realized that she didn't want to go home. She had already slept some, so it would be another night of staying awake and worrying until five. So she finished her drink, ordered another, and lit herself another smoke. But she didn't want to hang out here, either. None of her people were here—just a bunch of office workers not ready to go home, sprinkled with halfhearted partiers past their prime. She didn't see the Neapolitan or Doctor Shades or Jenny the Gent anywhere. Not even Telegram Sam, whose seat at the bar was probably molded to the shape of his ass by now. She put out her second cigarette and emptied the last of her drink, rattling the cubes in her glass to make sure the bastards weren't holding out on her.

Then a realization struck her so suddenly that she dropped ice onto her lap. She hadn't run her check yet! You *always* run a check right after a job! She pulled the tiny hardbound Coleridge out of her saddlebag of a purse, flipped open a page at random, and began reading:

DAY AFTER DAY, DAY AFTER DAY,
WE STUCK, NOR BREATH NOR MOTION;
AS IDLE AS A PAINTED SHIP,
UPON A PAINTED OCEAN.

"Babushka!" a young man's voice bellowed, startling her. "I hatt *hoped* I vould find you drinking wodka here!" Mara glared up at the skinny young man in black jeans and blue jean jacket that stood grinning at her like an idiot.

"Are you going to start counting things and chuckling like on Sesame Street?"

"No, I am being concerned friend from Mother Russia who sees dear Mara looking like *crazy* person, oh, *mwah*!" The Blemmye planted a fish-lipped kiss on her forehead, smearing her sunglasses, and sat down across from her. "Amaretto sour and some queso," he said in his normal voice before the waitress could finish materializing. He helped himself to one of Mara's cigarettes. "But seriously, what the hell, Mara? I know you look like Roseanne Rosannadanna whenever it rains, but that headscarf is insane."

"Roseanne who?"

"Never mind. Before your time," he said, even though he was younger than her. He nodded at the waitress and sipped his drink. "Was it something about that tall lady you came in with?" He dug around in his glass with the plastic swizzle stick, the unlit cigarette bobbing between his fingers.

"It was a Silhouette," she whispered.

The Blemmye's swizzle hand froze. "Jesus." He finally put the cigarette in his mouth, shook out another for her, stuck it in her mouth, and lit both with a Zippo that dated back to the Yalta Conference. Then, lacking anything better to say: "Jesus."

Mara sipped her greyhound. "Mike took care of it, apparently. The bouncer."

"Mara, you've been off your game lately. You need to take some time off. Take a vacation maybe."

"I can't," she said, staring down into her drink. "Between my rent and my bills and my credit cards. . . ." She had legal bills, too, but she didn't want to talk about those. She thought of something. "What's going to happen to the Silhouette, B?"

He seemed surprised. "The same thing that always happens. They'll put it into a blank white room until it dissipates down to a nub of meaning, then put an autistic kid in with it to soak up the meaning. Send the kid and a guardian out to put the displaced meaning back where it belongs, bippity boppity boo. Mara!" She had started crying, not even knowing why. He put his smooth hand over her malformed one and she drew back as though he had burned her.

"I'm sorry," she whispered. The Blemmye stood up, came around the table, and sat next to her. As the waitress laid the stone bowl of queso on the table, he held her and she cried. Finally, he brushed the tears out of her eyes with a napkin and lit two more cigarettes.

"Listen," he said, his arm still cradled around her shoulder. "I am *flush* with work. I am absolutely fucking *replete* with the stuff." He scooped queso-with-bits-of-sausage-in-it onto a tortilla chip and unhinged his jaw to eat it. "Mmh. But there's this job tomorrow night that might be good for you. It's not your usual thing, though. It's a little outside of your comfort zone."

"It's more *your* usual thing, right?" The Blemmye took the icky jobs, but he was a good drinking partner. And also loyal. Or perhaps she just had a thing for the men who took on the icky jobs. If he were ten years older than she was instead of ten years younger. . . ."Thank you, B., but I really don't—"

"Now hear me out! It's a young lady who stole money from her employer. Embezzled it. And her employer does all this charitable work that now goes right down the shitter because of it. She's a hard bitch, too. Never admitted to anything, represented herself at the trial, cracks jokes with the cops at the jail, remorseless—a real tough bitch. So." He hauled more queso to his mouth with a chip. "I mean, I do whatever job pays me the most, I don't give a shit. *You* know that. Punishment dreams, industrial espionage, dodgy seductions. I do what keeps Oklahoma Gas and Electric off my ass, you know? But *this* job? Mara, *this* dear lady has it coming."

"So it's a punishment dream."

The Blemmye licked cheese from his fingers, then wiped saliva off his fingers with a napkin. "I mean, we prefer to call em 'redemption dreams,' but yeah, it's the usual thing. Instead of just one dream, you'll go into her cell, where she'll be sleeping, with my agent. He's got all the chemistry stuff set up."

"Wait a minute, *cell*?"

"Yeah, she's at the jail just up the street there on Gray. *Any*way, the subject gets knocked out pretty deep, you go in like for any other weaving-type deal, but you *stay with* the dreamer. One dream dissipates, you hang out until the next one starts congealing, right? Three or four dreams that night, three or four the next, three or four the night after that. I would keep it to three nights if I were you. Four nights of this shit is a killer, especially if you're not used to it."

"And its just the same dream over and over?"

"Yeah, basically. Well, it's *episodes*, all in a loop. The setup that you use rewards her for accepting guilt and feeling shame, and it punishes her for not. She gets to wake up with warm fuzzy feelings if she accepts that she's done something wrong and that she needs to make amends. If she doesn't get to that point, then the dreams take her through another loop, another iteration, until she *does* accept that guilt. Loop after loop, until she realizes she deserves what she's gotten, realizes she needs to do something to make up for her crimes. I've already got the thing roughed out for you, and I can help you with some of the details, too. It'll be tomorrow night."

"It sounds sadistic."

The Blemmye shrugged. "Only if you enjoy doin it."

The Blemmye explained to her the details of the woman, who was named Sabine Mîeme, her crimes, and the sketch he was using to set up her Purgatory. "Last call," the waitress told them. Mara had a bad feeling about this job. She had a bad feeling about the Blemmye's agent, whom she met once before and who exuded disdain and evil. She had a bad feeling about everything.

As she gathered things into her purse, the Blemmye gripped one of her malformed hands tightly before she could pull it away. He looked in her eyes. "Listen. Mara. Honey, you got this. Okay?" Her heart was hammering. She didn't have this and she knew it. "You got this."

"Okay."

7.

She reached the county jail ten minutes late. The sun had just finished setting and the sky hadn't yet surrendered its last dark blue to the night. It had wanted to rain all day but had somehow failed to work up the nerve, so now the air was moist, hot, and oppressive. When she walked into the lobby, or foyer, or whatever you call that part of a jail, the Blemmye's agent was sitting on a blue plastic chair with chromium legs that would've looked more at home in a high school principal's office. The man was tall, thickset, and broad-shouldered, encased in a black suit that he seemed to have been born in, his silver hair and moustache sculpted with topiary-garden precision. With a start, she realized that he had been the man she had seen watching her at the bar last night. "Sorry I'm late," she panted, carefully keeping her hands shoved deep in her sweater pockets. The man's head swiveled up from the open file on his lap with reptilian slowness. This head movement completed, his eyes rotated upward with the slowness of a clock's minute hand until the twin nail-heads of his pupils were aimed at her face. *Don't show fear*, the Blemmmye had told her. *He can smell it like a dog.*

"Hello, Ms. Lee." He let first his head, then his pebble-colored eyes drift back down to his file folder. "You have had the opportunity, I take it, to study the subject's case file?" She nodded too quickly, too eagerly, her nearly spherical nest of hair frizzling and bobbing. "Good. Perhaps we could begin with the subject's name."

Mara tightened. "What about it?" She hadn't been quizzed on a job by someone since Hugh Tensile had trained her, before they'd even started dating.

"Recite. It." The agent's mouth sculpted each consonant with an icepick.

Mara took as deep a breath as she could manage without her baggy sweater giving her away. "Sabine Mîeme, 34, low-level manager for GlassDowns Consulting. Daughter, 19, lives just outside town, husband estranged. She's been indicted for embezzling, studied Chinese and Business Administration at Cornell University. Never showed any remorse, never showed any sense of guilt, told the judge at her trial to go fuck himself—should I go on?"

The corners of the agent's mouth widened an eighth of an inch without, however, moving upward. "No, thank you." He closed the case file and watched her. "I wonder if you could tell me what happened on your previous job. The one last night."

Mara swallowed before she could stop herself. Decided that frank honesty was the only way to go. "A Silhouette followed me out of the subject's dream."

"Don't you mean 'the *client's* dream?'"

Mara shrugged. "It was an odd contract. Someone else hired me to go into the man's dream." She licked her lips before she could stop herself. "I couldn't shake the Silhouette until I got to the bar. The bouncer, whatsisname, Mike, escorted it away."

"There is more to the story, of course."

"There always is."

He paused, dissatisfied. She wondered idly when he was going to offer her the chair across from him. "I wonder what caused your dreamer's mind to produce such a stable and vigorous Silhouette."

She shrugged too quickly. She was going to have to slow herself down to his rhythm or he was going to eat her alive. "I don't know."

"Don't you? A Silhouette, as I'm sure you're aware, results from some unnoticed parallel between the weaver's mind and the dreamer's. Some homologous complex, perhaps, some shared trauma. The surfeit of meaning resulting from this harmonic then latches onto the less-conscious parts of the weaver's mind and stows away, as it were, into the waking world." For the first time since she met him, he blinked. "And so?"

She thought about the Blemmye and was baffled. He always had nothing but nice things to say about this agent of his. Perhaps she was interacting with him all wrong. So how would the Blemmye be playing this encounter?

"I wonder," the agent continued, "if the problem might not relate in some way to recent events in your own life. Your subject's dog—female, lost, beloved—might perhaps have triggered a few associations, *n'est-ce pas*? And if you follow this line of thinking a bit further, I believe you will understand my concern. Here, this evening, we have a young woman of approximately your own age. She has family issues that will not be entirely foreign to you. She is in some amount of legal trouble, with which you can also relate, I suppose." He looked at her without moving, as though he would be perfectly comfortable observing her embarrassed silence all night. If this were a dream, there would be no trouble at all: she would simply do a character. So why not make the same play here?

She put on the Blemmye. She let her jaw scoot forward half an inch, let her hands out of her pockets, and straightened her back, which she hadn't even realized was bent. She very slowly and purposely swiveled her head to the left, taking in the two obese cops chatting behind a pane of Plexiglass. She swiveled her head right and saw the now-black sky and the nondescript lawyers' offices across the street. Then she looked back at the agent. Looking into his eyes would imply equivalence, would imply that he was on her level. But he was seated, he was elderly, and he was being an asshole. She instead fixed her gaze on the space between his eyes and his eyebrows. His gaze belonged below hers. When she spoke, her voice had a power that it never had in waking life. "You pretty good at hiding things? Because I don't see any other weavers lurking around. So since I'm the one *doing* this job, any chance we could get started?" She could feel, without looking, that the cops had stopped chatting and were now watching. She felt her own eyes gimlet their way into the agent's eyelids, felt her jaw and shoulders relax. The Blemmye is always relaxed because he has no habitual patterns, she realized. He simply gives what he gets. Now that the agent's storm of disrespectful bullshit had subsided, her body was calm, ready to reflect back at him whatever he planned to hit her with next.

Amazingly, he hit her with a sunny smile, his ribcage nearly allowing a desert-dry chuckle to leave his body. "Please," he said, gesturing at the chair across from him. "Do sit down. We've a few matters to discuss before going back to Miss Mîeme's cell. The Blemmye says that you are experienced, trustworthy, and effective. I merely want to make sure that you yourself would agree. A lack of confidence translates almost directly in dreams into a lack of talent. But I see now that you are confident."

"Uh huh." Thankfully, it was still her version of the Blemmye talking, and not her.

"So let's discuss the job."

"Oh, well, let's don't *rush into* anything." The agent actually gave a slight chuckle at this, and it was worse than any silence from him so far.

8.

The lady cop was irritable, charmless, and had a voice like hard plastic being tortured, but something about her commanded obedience. "Empty yer pockets. Belt, purse, smokes, jewerry, everything goes inna bins." Mara and the agent emptied their pockets and left purse and case file in cheap plastic tubs the color of bureaucracy. The small hardback tumbled out of Mara's saddlebag of a purse. The agent did something that, on someone else's face, might have resembled a smile instead of a chitinous grimace.

"Coleridge. I hadn't thought you a literary type."

"It's what I use for checks." He blinked at her. "Turn to a page at random, read a bit of it, look away for a few seconds, then reread the passage a second time, word-by-word, to make sure it's the same. To make sure you aren't dreaming."

"Ah."

"This way," the cop said irritably. She led Mara and the agent down a hallway running between two rows of empty cells. The concrete floor was lit by a series of bare bulbs in metal cones, the circles of jaundiced concrete separated from their neighbors by strips of less jaundiced concrete. The cop went ahead of them to the last cell on the right, unlocked the cage door, and let them inside. "She's out pretty hard," the cop explained. "One of you can come get me when yer finished." The cop waddled back up the hallway.

The agent watched Mara carefully as she first caught sight of the prisoner. Sabine Mîeme was sleeping on a thin mattress laid over a metal cot, her back to them, a tangled mass of curly dark hair haloing her head and neck. Over her was a blanket that didn't have any definite idea of what color it wanted to be. "Sabine Mîeme," the agent murmured. "Our embezzler, spy, and what have you. Have a look." Mara strode into the cell. She looked down at the sleeping woman. For some reason, she couldn't help thinking of when she used to wake up her daughter on school mornings. The girl's hair was always a tangled nest, like her mother's, like this woman's. Her breath was slow and regular, like this woman's. But she was not here to wake Ms. Mîeme: instead, she was here to make her sleep more useful to her captors. More "redemptive."

Mara dug in her bag for the vial, the doll, the handkerchief. Looking at the captive, she had a vision, or a dream, or whatever normal people call it when they have something like a dream when they aren't asleep. She saw herself spooning the prisoner, their hair, face, clothes, and posture identical, dead to the world in endless sleep, the cell door clanging shut on them forever. It was like looking at another version of her life that had been sculpted and stuck into her life. A picture inside a picture, a novel that shows up inside itself, being read by one of its characters. The French had some kind of word for it that Hugh had taught her when he used to prattle on about Godard and Robbe-Grillet and all that other shit. What was it?

She knew she couldn't take this job. If this woman was going to have punishment, or redemption, she should be able to see it coming, be a part of it. Mara put her gear back into her bag and stepped closer to the sleeping woman. Even in the dim light filtering through the bars from the hallway, she could just see the woman's ear and the curve of one cheek. She was startled by the agent gripping her arm and whispering violently: "*Ms. Lee.*" She pointed out to the hallway. Without looking at him, she began walking that way herself. *Mise en abîme*, that was the word. Once they were outside the cell she turned to face the agent, whose jaw seemed to have grown several new layers of disapproving tendon.

"What's wrong?" he demanded.

"I'm sorry. That woman in there looks just like my daughter."

"She's 34 years old!"

Mara ignored him. "If I go into her dreams, there's no telling what I might bring back with me. I can't do it." She didn't tell him that the woman lying there on a prison cot also reminded her a good deal of herself. Right down to the jail cell and cot, if she were honest. She shivered at old ghosts.

He looked at her with expressionless lizard eyes and walked back up the hallway. "Officer!" he barked, his voice ringing the bars on both sides of the hall.

As herself, she would have apologized several times, but she was still partly playing the Blemmye. She kept silent. Shit happens. Too bad if the agent can't deal. When they reached the foyer, the agent turned to her. "Ms. Lee, I suppose you realize that you are not the only weaver able to carry out jobs of this variety. Even if the Blemmye already has plans, I have other resources which I can bring to bear. One weaver in particular, though blunt in his approach, can handle this job quite effectively. Your failure this evening is at most an inconvenience to me. But last night, Ms. Lee, you led a Silhouette back into the waking world. Tonight, you have turned your back on a job which you led me to believe you could carry out. I am very much afraid, Ms. Lee, that these repeated failings may lead you to some difficulties finding work in the future."

She got closer to him. Closer. And then she saw it. The hard line of the mouth, only partly camouflaged by the white moustache. The odd set of the shoulders, never fully relaxing, always on guard. Of course. Even the stupid puns, the anagrams, the never-ending bullshit wordplay. Of course. She smiled and put her hand on the agent's shoulder. Let him know with her eyes what she had realized. Put her head closer to whisper in his ear.

The blaring of the telephone shattered the moment and caused her to open her eyes to blinding glare. "Fuck," she mumbled, shielding her face. What the hell time was it? She spent a moment figuring out whether the noise was a fire alarm, her alarm clock, or the phone. Fumbled the phone from her bedside table. "Hello?"

The voice at the other end was a man's, quiet and devoid of personality. "May I please speak with Miss Mara Lee?"

"Speaking."

"A friend of yours gave me your number, Ms. Lee. My name is Droste and I'm Superintendent of Jails and Prisons in this county. I believe you and an associate were going to visit our jail this evening for a sort of meeting with one of our inmates?"

Mara thought for a moment. It was difficult. "Yeah, yuh, yes yes, that's right."

The man cleared his throat again. "Well, I am, um, sorry to inform you that this meeting will no longer be taking place. It turns out that, um, the prisoner has ended her own life during the night."

The silence rang like a bell. "I see."

"And so, therefore, um, your services will no longer be required."

"Well. I'm sorry to hear it."

"Indeed. Indeed. I am, of course, sorry also. To be telling you. And, um. Well."

"Thanks for calling."

"You're welcome, Miss Lee. Goodbye."

She hung up and tried to remember the dream that the phone had interrupted. She had been visiting her daughter's school, perhaps. A bad meeting at the principal's office. Had that been it? She vaguely remembered Hugh Tensile being there. Benson, Tensile, whatever. She considered taking down her dream diary and recording the odd scraps that she could remember. It was always good to take everything down, to keep an inventory. But the phone had left so little of the dream to her that it didn't seem worth the bother. The person from Porlock, she thought. The dream was gone.

Knowing her dreams, that was probably just as well.

9.

As afternoon shaded into evening, Mara finally got up the gumption to leave the house. She didn't particularly want to leave the house, but then again, she didn't particularly want to stay at home, either. She wanted to not exist so much anymore. She wanted to tell her daughter how things got so screwed up, wanted to watch a dumb old movie with her, wanted to ask her about her day, about school, about why she looked sad. Is it your father?

She knew she couldn't fill another sleepless night with lazing around and moping, though she was practiced at both, so she got dressed and made her way over to the Glueshine. On the way, she passed a group of little kids taking swats at a piñata hanging from a tree. The piñata looked enormous and dense. Though the wind ruffled the fringes of white paper covering it, it did not sway the piñata itself at all, and even when one of the kids got in an especially good whack, the piñata barely swung. Instead of being multicolored like most piñatas she'd seen, this one was entirely white, and instead of being shaped like a burro or a star, this one was shaped like a boxy sheep with a pink bow tied around its neck and a delicate pink ribbon tucked behind one ear. Only the narrowest thread attached it to its tree branch. Between the immense weight of the sheep-piñata and the repeated thwackings from the children, Mara was astonished that the thread didn't simply snap.

She got to the bar just as the sun was sinking toward the horizon and a light sprinkle of cool rain was starting. She was glad she'd decided to take the umbrella after all, and even more glad that there was going to be some rain. It had been unmercifully muggy these last two days. As she walked into the bar, she was nauseated by the yellow, buttery sunlight straining its way through the greasy windows and bathing everything in headache. She wished some more cloud would come in. Something about rain and sunlight at the same time made the sunlight more painful.

As she passed the bar, she saw two women at a small table, one of whom looked just like Jenny the Gent. Jesus, she hadn't seen Jenny since—but the smile froze on Mara's face, withered, and she replaced it with no-expression. Jenny's eyes had darted up to Mara's face for a brief moment, flickered in recognition, then turned away, her jaw hardening. Mara pulled her own eyes away and pretended not to notice, pretended not to recognize a woman she'd been friends with for seven years, eight, and who now had no more use for her than for old coffee grounds. She swallowed the lump in her throat and took one of the booths by the window. Probably the same one she'd taken the night before, she realized. Two nights before? No, the night before. Like most weavers, she found it hard to keep waking life and dreaming life in separate little watertight compartments. As she sat smoking and trying not to look over at Jenny and watching the sprinkling rain and the sunset out the big window, she heard a young girl's chuckle that sounded familiar. Looking across the bar, she saw an older man she thought she recognized from somewhere sitting across the table from her Silhouette. She jumped. The two were chuckling happily at some private joke. The man put his hand over the Silhouette's—her hand was pale and smooth, with narrow, nimble fingers perfect for piano, violin, or scalpel—and she placed her other hand over his, still laughing. She was beautiful, Mara realized, a pang of jealousy stabbing through her. That's my Silhouette, she found herself thinking. *Mine.*

"Mara! Are you just gonna ignore your Uncle Sam here or what?!"

Mara turned and saw the chubby older man with the Pirates cap and the black T-shirt whose words had been eroded into cuneiform by decades of careless laundering. "Sam! How did I not see you? I walked right by your seat!" She stood and gave Telegram Sam a big hug, and he squeezed the breath out of her and sat down at her table. "How have you been?" He shrugged, gestured vaguely with his cigarette, and grunted. The waitress plunked down a tumbler of Jameson in front of him and he gave her a nod and a rubbery-mouthed smile.

Mara found herself looking back over at the older man and the Silhouette. They were chatting warmly as the man set up the board and pieces for a game of chess. Sam followed her gaze and guessed her thoughts. "Yeah, I never thought I'd see the day they'd domesticate a Silhouette. Seems to me like that'd be dangerous."

"Apparently not."

"Yeah, apparently not." Sam stubbed out his menthol, gulped down some whiskey, and belched quietly. "I heard you had one of those. A Silhouette I mean. You okay, honey?"

Mara shook her head. "I don't know. Just off my game, I guess. The worst part is, I had to drag her up here for them to deal with and somebody saw me, so now the guy thinks I'm a kidnapper. He came up here yesterday and tried to get the bouncer to call the cops."

Sam chortled. "Mike? Yeah, good luck getting that guy to do anything but go to the gym and glare." They chuckled as the waitress brought tortilla chips that hadn't been asked for. "I got a job you might like, honey. Just exactly your cup of tea. One of those healing dreams. But the thing is, though, that it's for *later tonight*. You interested?"

Mara shrugged. "I guess so."

Sam peered at her. Drank his whiskey. Peered at her some more. "You're looking peaked, honey. How long since you seen sunlight?" She laughed. "I'm serious! You look like shit!"

Mara sighed. "So what's the job?"

He eyed her some more, realized this was none of his business, and finished his whiskey. "There's this *fella*," he began. As he talked, she realized that she was starving. She ordered cheese fries with bacon on them that they both devoured as he showed her a floor plan to the house, explained the man's life, described the job. The sprinkle outside was turning into a hellish downpour, the sky a grey stone, thunder booming louder and closer. Mara had trouble following what Sam was telling her. She was distracted by her memory of Jenny the Gent snubbing her. Fair-weather friends. Not like Sam, or the Blemmye either, for that matter. Sam was friends with everybody, of course. And the Blemmye had always been loyal to her, a good friend, no matter what, even right up to—

A blinding flash, a murderous blast of thunder that rattled the windows, the lights in the bar strobing. Everybody jumped and Mara instinctively put her hand over her chest to calm her heart down. "Jesus Christ," somebody muttered, plainly audible in the sudden silence, and a couple of patrons chuckled nervously. The light steadied. As the rain went up a gear, the dull chatter in the bar resumed hesitantly. Sam's eyes glittered almost like a sober person's and he held a middle finger up to the sky.

"You missed, asshole!" He and Mara laughed for almost a full minute, then went back to their floorplans and cheese fries. She was glad to be talking to a real friend, finally. Jenny snubbing her, and before that, the Blemmye giving her that bum job that was all wrong for her. What could he have been *thinking*?

She had drunk too much, and too quickly. Her head swam and she excused herself to go to the bathroom. She looked at the pale, frizzle-headed girl-woman staring at her in the mirror. The girl with messed-up hands, the pariah. This job, at least, seemed like something more her speed, something she could carry out, literally, in her sleep.

Hopefully.

10.

The storm had calmed itself down to a mist, and night was just settling in. Mara had left the bar confident that she could navigate to the dreamer's house easily, but she had taken a wrong turn at some point and now had to backtrack. The right angles and stable landmarks of the waking world were not her forte, and she was still trying to shake off her hazy-headedness from the bar. Stupid to eat so much and drink so much right before a job. She probably shouldn't even have taken the job, felt so tired and tipsy that she might as well have been dreaming already. She was half-tempted to drag the Coleridge out of her purse and do a check right there on the curb. Perhaps things would have been better if she had taken that job at the prison, with the embezzler, hadn't gotten scared and run away. She would have completed a job, even though it was outside her normal skill-set. It might have gotten her some respect, at least, from old friends who otherwise snubbed her, wouldn't talk to her. She hadn't done herself any favors by turning the job down.

She found the right street and turned down it in what she hoped was the right direction, then realized something. She hadn't turned down the job with that Mîeme woman at all. The woman had hung herself. Mara had never even gone down to the jail. She found herself chuckling at her own confusion. It was that dream about talking to her daughter's principal at the school, *that's* what it was. She was confusing *that* dream with how she had imagined the job at the jail might turn out. She had been scared to meet that one agent, and it had triggered memories of meeting with her daughter's principal, like in that dream, or when she had *actually* talked to her daughter's principal, after Hugh had—*anyway*, she had never been any good at distinguishing real life from dreams at all. Hugh Tensile had been an asshole at the end, had done some things that he probably regretted, but that was one thing he was always right about. No doubt about it. She felt dark memories crowd her, curdled pasts, grey cubes with unpleasant memory-pictures in them. And then she saw the lights from the cop car.

Mara stopped, turned innocently. Two cops, one a short Latina with a rigid face and the other a tall, densely built Caucasian. The big white man got out of the car. "Everything all right, ma'am?" He moseyed around the front of the car and paused in front of Mara. His badge, she saw, read HILHEN. What an odd name.

"Been better, been worse," she said, chuckling nervously, her hands stuffed rigidly into her pockets. Then she remembered that cops don't like hands in pockets, reluctantly pulled them out, dropping the umbrella from the crook of her elbow in the process. "Well, crap."

"You live around here?" Hilhen asked. She nodded, trying to pick up her umbrella without making any sudden moves. Cops don't find it suspicious when people are nervous around them, she knew—quite the reverse—and a poker face is sometimes needed. But when someone seems reticent or only gives half of an answer, cops are trained to dig deeper. She would have to be a tranquil pool of deep, clear water.

"Whereabouts?"

She pointed, not sure whether it was in the right direction. "About a half a mile, maybe even almost a mile, that way."

Hilhen nodded as the Latina—GUEST, her badge said—observed Mara expressionlessly. Her voice didn't seem to move her lips much and had more in common with Morse code than English. "Got a license, ma'am?"

"Um, sure." Mara dug through the contents of her saddlebag-purse, praying the cops wouldn't see her unusual custom-made inhaler, her quasi-legal cannister of expired pepper spray, her three little bottles of odd chemicals, or worst of all, her mare's-nest of zip-ties. "At last," she chuckled with a tight grin, handing Guest the laminated card. The cop brought it to her face, handed it back.

The man spoke. "Are you coming from your house, or going to?"

"Um, neither. I'm just walking around and thinking about stuff. I just had a drink at that bar up the road. I was trying to clear my head." She got an odd scratch in her throat, and clearing it out made a loud noise that got their attention. She saw their attention-faces recover into poker-faces and knew she was in trouble. Soon they would ask questions that wouldn't be good for her, or would call in and learn about her record. The large man gave half a nod.

"You go to that same bar last night, ma'am?"

Last night, last night. As usual, she was having trouble teasing apart what had happened today, last night, the night before last, in waking, in dreams, and in her most recent dream-assignment. She decided to go with statistics. "Yes," she said, a little too suddenly.

The Latina's voice startled her. "These are not hard questions, Ms. Lee."

Cops only notice oddities, and they don't know which oddities come from a horrible life, which come from a confusing life, and which come from them catching you in a series of lies. "It's been sort of a long day," Mara said lamely.

"So about one or two last night, early this morning, you went to the Silent Hug?"

Mara was baffled. "The what?"

"Your bar."

"The Glueshine?"

The big white cop gave his partner a slight smile. "You're using the old name for it, before it changed ownership." He turned his rubber-mask face back to Mara and his amusement vanished. "Yeah. The Glueshine."

Why were they fishing for a specific time? And *had* she really been at the bar last night? Wasn't last night when she had gone to that meeting with—but no, that had been a dream, that's right. She had been talking to the Blemmye about a job. Or, no, that couldn't be right. It had been Sam she'd been talking to. Jesus, what a time to have Mara Brain. "I guess it was about one or two. Yes, because it was an hour before closing." She felt triumphant. She'd found a way to justify her hesitation—she had just been fishing around for the exact time. But she felt very much like a frizzle-haired problem child in front of these two, and their faces were all dark attention. She swallowed hard before remembering that that's what guilty people do.

Hilhen spoke quietly, smoothly. "What were you doing before then?"

She managed not to swallow again. "Um." Looked up and to the left to mimic someone trying to remember something. "Well, I had just finished up some work for somebody. I'm a weaver, I do various odd jobs, you know." She saw that the cops were both as still as lizards, and she knew. They were wanting to know about the Silhouette and what the man on the second floor had seen. Had *he* seen the zip-ties? "I ran into an old friend of mine on the way there and we chatted for a few minutes," she finished lamely. The mist had been thickening without her noticing and was now a lazy drizzle.

"And was this a boyfriend?" Hilhen asked.

"Nuh, no sir. A girlfriend, it was a girlfriend." Mara noticed that the cops had, by half steps and quarter steps, gradually positioned themselves so that they had her in a sort of pincer, her back mere inches from the door of the cop car, as though worried she might try to run away. She managed again not to swallow, started to nervously stuff her hands into her pockets, stopped herself. Hilhen spoke again.

"Did the two of you enter the Glueshine together?"

"No, she didn't." Mara heard how thin and breathless her voice sounded, took in some more air to fortify it. She was going to need a strategy, fast. "No, she, uh, came up on the elevator with me to finish our chat, you know, but then she went back down because she had to get home." Being herself was not working, and she was getting to the point where even three-quarter truths weren't satisfying these people. Her answers to their questions were automatically spinning her a web of suspicion, a jail cell, a burial. Things that only happen to people who are actually guilty. She tried to meet the cops' blank eyes as best she could, took a breath, felt grateful for her baggy sweater.

"Your friend's name?" Guest barked, startling her.

"Emily," she blurted out before realizing she'd done it. Her daughter's name. It was a good lie.

The bulky white man paused, looked down at the toe of his shoe, considering. But cops never consider anything. They don't have to. That's what their training is for. A cop pretending to think is really a cop preparing to pounce. "You and this Emily person. The two of you didn't get out of the elevator together on any floor?"

They have me, she realized. She felt like she'd been punched in the stomach, like when she had found out about the Blemmye, Jesus that had hurt. The breath fled her in a ragged gasp and her head fell. She'd been in this kind of moment before and she knew all its hidden contours, all its secret flows, even knew what would happen next. She said "Um" to make the future give her another few seconds before clapping shut around her and dragging her off to the jail down on Gray Street. Their witness on the second floor had seen everything. Including, probably, zip-ties from the same batch that she had right now in her purse.

When Guest spoke again, her voice was gentle and warm. "So she got out of the elevator with you before the two of you reached the bar. On the second floor. Is that right?"

Their conversation would become leisurely now. They'd help her to answer their questions, all of which would be easy, and it would end with her going into the back of their car for a little ride. Mara swallowed hard. She did not want to take that ride, so she rolled the dice. Giggled nervously. "Jeez, um, I'm in some sort of trouble now, huh? Um." She put her hand over her mouth. She let her body radiate every guilty signal she'd been bottling up for the last five minutes. She took a deep, deep breath, closed her eyes, and let all her tension leave her body. Suddenly, her blank, relaxed mind gave her an image: Sabine Mîeme standing in front a judge's bench and telling him to go fuck himself. The image was so funny she half-chuckled, which made her look even more criminal. She opened her eyes, relieved that she could breathe again, and looked at the two cops. "So, yeah. Emily *did* get off of the elevator with me on, um, on the second floor." Mara cleared her throat noisily again. The cops kept waiting, watching the rabbit run at their jaws. "I know that floor is private property and that you're not supposed to go there after hours but me and Emily used to have these fun adventures together back in high school and it had been forever since I'd seen her last and I remembered how we'd gone up there one time to the second floor and seen a couple of people working and mooned them and then gone up to the bar upstairs to the women's bathroom until they went away and so we were just, um, reminiscing about that." She swallowed. "So, yeah. I'm sorry. This guy was up there and he saw us, and we probably kind of startled him." The drizzle was working itself up to a proper rain and she remembered her umbrella, then her cigarettes. Clumsily, she managed to get the umbrella over her head and a lit cigarette into her mouth. All the while, she felt their eyes pressing into her. Like dough. "I had missed her so much, and we used to have so much *fun* together." Shut up, she told herself. Don't give them the story. Make them put it together out of the pieces you give them or they'll realize it's manufactured.

"And why did she scream?"

Emily was so involved thinking about rain, her cigarette, and her imaginary friend that she'd forgotten about the Silhouette's screaming. "What? Who?"

"Emily. She screamed and she tried to get away from you. Why?"

"We both did. Screamed, I mean. We were startled by the guy we saw, and we maybe wanted to give him kind of a scare, too. We just both became high school kids again for a minute, I guess."

Guest's face was like granite. "She screamed 'Daddy,'" she told Mara. "The man on the second floor *heard* it."

Mara laughed, her mouth open. "'Daddy,'" she said, her hand over her mouth. "Oh, he *wishes* she said that!" She tried to laugh some more, sucked in too much smoke at once, and fell into a hacking cough. "'Daddy!'"

The cops relaxed now, even had half-smiles. It had all been a misunderstanding. They told her to stay off the second floor in the future, and to be sure and call a cab if she needed one. She waved as they got back into their car and drove away. A cab, she thought. Jesus, were they ninety? Why not an Uber?

Mara let her heart and breathing settle down and felt the sweat soak the inside of her shirt even as the rain soaked the outside. She'd be seeing the cops again, she knew. Maybe because of the squirrelly-ass job tonight, maybe as they dug deeper into the whole Silhouette thing. She remembered the face her lawyer had given her as the jury had left for deliberation. Hopeless, apologetic, ready to move on to the next case. She walked up the street a few dozen yards to a dark area midway between two streetlamps. Walking back from the curb there was a well-manicured bush, almost spherical. She knelt behind it in the wet grass and vomited, rocked back and forth a few moments, vomited again.

It was time to get to work.

11.

After washing her mouth off in a mud puddle, she got her bearings. Talking with the cops had gotten her all turned around, and now that it was completely dark, everything looked different. She finally found the client's street—a short cul-de-sac lined with well-trimmed hedges, with two houses on each side and a fifth, larger house at the end—his. She shouldn't have taken the job tonight. Tired, tipsy, and still frazzled from the cops, she started down the street.

She couldn't believe how lucky she'd been with those cops. They seemed ready to pounce, but then they had let her go with a smile. Maybe the spirit of Sabine Mîeme had helped her with that vision of cussing out the judge. Maybe confessing to the lesser crime of trespassing had done the trick. But things like this don't simply drop out of sight. They sink, burbling, into the dark muck, then come floating back to the surface, larger than ever. Maybe the accountant on the second floor would make more noise, or maybe the cops would go into the Glueshine some night looking for her and instead find the Silhouette and talk to it instead. And there were more than enough people who wouldn't mind handing her over to the authorities at any opportunity. She could feel her various failings and weaknesses and mistakes sending out tendrils into the world, could feel the various cops and FBI agents and bureaucrats brushing by these tendrils and becoming *interested*. She could feel the hard, narrow cot beneath her, the stone and iron all around.

Maybe she should just tell them what happened and hope for the best. She'd been somewhere she shouldn't have, had done things she shouldn't have done. She-

"Bullshit!" she said aloud, startling herself. Bullshit. She'd gotten a Silhouette and had handled it pretty well, considering. She was no goddam criminal. As she walked up the driveway to the side of the client's house, she felt her jaw tightening, as though she were still playing the Blemmye character she'd done earlier for—who had that been, exactly? "Bullshit," she whispered. She'd made mistakes, had broken the law once or twice, but she was no worse than anyone else. Tears of anger burned her eyes as she walked around to the house's side yard. There was a tall wooden fence with a tree growing just this side of it. A good climbing tree. She talked shit about herself because she was used to it. She'd had plenty of time, god knows, with Hugh God Almighty Tensile forever telling when she'd fucked up and how she'd fucked up and how he knew better and how stupid and confused and crazy she was, every fucking day. Every fucking night. Every fucking opportunity, like she was 20 years younger instead of 10. She scraped the side of her leg against the bark of the birch tree and whispered a curse, the blood surprising her. Then she got to the top of the tree, looked over the fence, and got an even worse surprise: there was a tall man with blonde hair in a suit wandering the backyard, a machine pistol dangling carelessly from his shoulder.

Mara half-fell from the tree, her fall softened by thick mud. She slapped her hand over her mouth to stifle a cry. She froze. There was a knothole in one of fence's planks and she chanced a look. The guard was looking over his shoulder at the tops of the two birch trees, one growing on each side of the fence. Then, as the rain started again, he turned back away from the fence, the trees, and Mara. Mara backed away, fishing the umbrella out of her enormous bag again. To her right, a loud jangling on the front porch surprised her—a windchime, made of white tubes that might as well have been bone. She held her hand over her chest and steadied her breathing. Kneeling in the darkness by the porch, screened from the street by ruler-perfect hedges, she considered. She could get into a locked house, that was no problem. She even had the four-digit security code for the back door. But there was a guard by the back door, and the other two doors of the house had different codes, neither of which she had. She clumsily unfolded her umbrella, nearly dropping both it and her bag into the mud in the process. A gust of wind tugged at the umbrella, yanked it, snapped one of its ribs so that its bat-fluttering membrane whipped back and forth in the frenzied rain. "Fuck!" she hissed as the flapping umbrella-rib slashed her cheek. She threw the umbrella down and it sank partway into the mud, its broken wing-bone jutting toward the sky.

The sky let loose, pouring an ocean of water diagonally. There was no other way into the house, she realized. She had just one option: she'd have to dig under the mud with her misshapen hands, then tunnel across to the basement. She didn't like the idea, but it was the only possible way. She knelt in a large patch of soft mud, free of any troublesome plants or stones. She'd been so strong. She'd done so much. For Emily *and* for Hugh. She'd tried her best, and things had taken some turns. But she'd tried. Maybe it's best to let go now. Not worry so much, not work so much. Let things take their course. Go to the police. Tell them the full story. Apologize. With that, perhaps, she might know peace. Might even find her way toward a fresh start, a new life.

She sighs, looking down at her reflection in the puddle in front of her. With her hair being blown by the wind and the puddle being splashed with rain, she thinks for a moment that she is looking at her daughter, at Emily. So, so much like her mother. Mara feels the need to cry fill her chest. Feels the need to give up fill her throat.

"No," she whispers, shaking her head slowly. She concentrates on her breathing, the rain on her skin, the circular ripples in front of her. She takes her hands out of her pockets and stares at them grimly. It will take half the night, she realizes, but she knows that she can get into the house. She'll tunnel in and she'll do the job and then she'll go on to the next thing. And the next and the next and the next and the next. No time to dwell on the past. There's work to be done.

Setting her jaw, she takes the massive spoons that grow from her wrists instead of hands, plunges them into the soft earth, and begins digging.

About the Author

Daniel Dickson-LaPrade lives in Pittsburgh, Pennsylvania with his family and a number of smallish animals.